The National Healthy Marriage Institute is a social enterprise organization dedicated to developing products and services that can help couples form and sustain healthy marriages.

We would like to thank the talented authors who contributed to this volume. Without their efforts this tool would not be available to you.

Copyright 2009 by The National Healthy Marriage Institute. All rights reserved. No part of this book may be reproduced or transmitted in any form or by any means, electronic or mechanical, including but not limited to, photocopying, recording, or by any information storage and retrieval system, without permission in writing from the publisher, A&E Family Publishers (866) 321- 2665.

Significant bulk order discounts are available. Please contact A&E Family Publishers for more details.

Photo credits: Comstock & Eyewire

Ounce of Prevention:

Short Stories to Keep Your Marriage Healthy and Happy

Index

Introduction	4
Education of Rachel	6
Growing a Marriage Garden	18
Creating a Soul Mate	31
What's in a Name	40
Growing Back Together Again	50
Why Can't You Just Say "I Love You"	58

Bonus Section

Healthy Marriage Pamphlet Series	67
Track it to a Habit Log	71
Strengthening My Marriage Plan	73
Appreciation Journal	79
Mountain Home Base Resource List	96

Introduction

An ounce of prevention is worth more than a pound of cure. We have all heard this saying before but what does it mean for our marriages?

On the day couples get married they almost all share the same dream: a lifelong, healthy and happy marriage. Yet within a few years that dream has been shattered for many by divorce. In fact, by the time the couples lives on this earth come to an end, less than 50% will have achieved their dream.

So why is it that over 50% of couples never achieve the dream they share on their wedding day? For nearly all of them it is because they fail to learn and follow a few simple rules and insights couples in healthy and happy marriages follow as demonstrated by research.

The next question you might ask is, with the consequences of divorce being so horrific for the couple and their children, why don't more couples learn and implement these skills and insights? The answer is somewhat complicated but in essence it is because almost all couples are <u>currently</u> satisfied with their marital relationship. If you are satisfied with the way things are, you are not very likely to use your time and energy to prevent problems you think will never happen to you. A common thought is "It will never happen to us because we are different." Everyday people who had the exact same thought are now filling out divorce papers.

Unfortunately, the majority of the couples motivated to take the time and effort to learn these skills and insights do so because the pain level in their marital relationship is so high. They are willing to do just about anything to relieve it. This is much like a person with a severe sunburn. They are very willing to apply just about any cream to their body to alleviate the pain, but just a few short hours before thought it would be too much hassle to apply sunscreen.

We have created this book to help you apply sunscreen to your marriage. While each short story is fun to read on its own, we hope you will take the time to complete the worksheet created for each short story. The worksheets have been designed to help you start applying sunscreen to your marital relationship by implementing the skills and insights researchers have found can help couples form and sustain healthy marriages.

The following story illustrates the benefit of applying these principles. Two farmers lived next to each other. One farmer plowed his fields, but would never manage to get around to planting and nurturing them. His neighbor would not only plow, plant, and nurture, but at the end of the season would harvest a bounteous crop and enjoy the fruits of his labors. If you only read these short stories and never implement what you learn, you will reap the same benefits as the farmer who plowed but never planted. On the other hand, if you choose to implement what you learn, then you can reap the rewards of a lifelong healthy and happy marriage.

What kind of spouse do you want and what are YOU doing to become like that?

The Education of Rachel

Kendall was a 40 something investment specialist, and I was her hairdresser. She got her hair done every six weeks, her nails every three; I did them both. She tipped well, which I appreciated. But the best part about Kendall was that she listened to me. She really seemed to understand my problems. Usually as a hairdresser, I play the part of therapist. I listen to women go on about their kids, their mothers-in-law, their attempts to diet. Sometimes there's a juicy piece of gossip that involves another client of the salon, so it's not always a total bore. But with Kendall, it was different. I found myself opening up to her. She didn't seem to mind. If she did, I'm sure she would have told me. She wasn't afraid to speak her mind, when she actually spoke. She listened to me until one day. That was the day she taught me about myself.

My name is Rachel. I married Luke Walker (and no, his middle name is not Sky) two years ago. We are both 29. He does computer work for a large company here in town. We don't have kids yet, and we're in no rush either. We met on a blind date. For him, it was love at first sight. For me, it was a month before I knew I was hooked. Tall, dark, handsome, thoughtful; a strong, quiet type. When we were dating, Luke was such a gentleman. Opening doors, letting me pick the movies, and stuff like that. He was sweet. He brought me flowers sometimes, or he'd get my favorite ice cream (chocolate caramel nut), and sometimes he'd bring me lunch from my favorite Chinese place down the street. He isn't quite the talker that I am, and I think that's why we hit it off. As they say, opposites attract! We dated for about a year before he proposed, and were married six months later. Things were so great at the beginning. We got a cute apartment, bought nice furniture, entertained friends, went out to eat all the time, and I got the new car. Marriage wasn't the "big adjustment" everyone said it would be. It was exactly what I wanted: great guy, great apartment, great furniture, great car, great friends. Life was great! I was great, and I thought he was too. How quickly all that greatness changed.

Luke makes pretty good money at his job. Computer nerds always do. I do pretty well at the salon. I'm one of the top stylists, and my appointment book is always full. Money is not an issue to me, but that is right where Luke started changing things. I have a job where my clothes, hair, and accessories are my uniform. I like to stay updated, so I need to shop frequently. We also live in a big city, so the apartment isn't cheap. Luke wanted to live in the 'burbs, but I fell in love with this historic apartment building downtown. So we live downtown. Like I said, we both make good money, so I didn't see the problem. About six months after we were married, Luke started complaining that I spend too much money. Did I really need another $90 pair of jeans when I had a drawer full of them? He said I needed to cut back on my clothes, and that we needed to stop eating out. He said that since I insisted on living in an expensive apartment, and financing all the furniture, I needed to buckle down so we could pay it all off. Luke wants to save money to buy a house, and said we should set up a budget. He wasn't nice about it at all. I felt

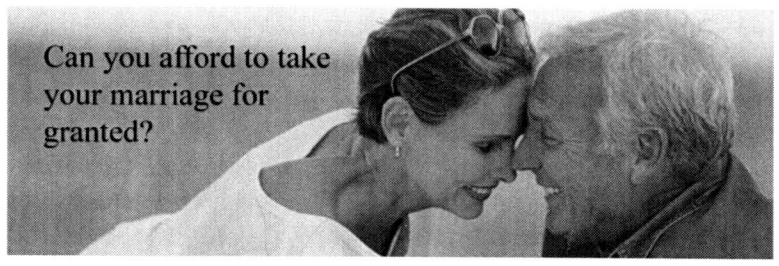

Can you afford to take your marriage for granted?

like he was picking on me. It seemed like everyday he would tell me I need to quit buying this or that, and that he should put me on an allowance. Excuse me...an allowance? I'm not 10 years old.

Since he was so into pointing out my 'faults', I started paying more attention to his. I said before he is a quiet type. That is the most annoying thing in the world. I want to talk things out. He makes a grand pronouncement, then won't talk it over. He doesn't listen to me. I try to explain things to him, and he won't listen. I told my best friend Kristin (she also works at the salon) about Luke's new money plan. She thought he was being ridiculous, and told him that to his face when he brought me lunch that afternoon. I love Kristin! When my mom asked me how things were going, I told her. She didn't say much, but didn't like that Luke was treating me with so little respect.

Then, Luke started working overtime. He said it was because of debt problems that we needed the extra money. Right. I think he doesn't want to be around me. I don't want to be around him either. All he does is talk about money, and I hate that. So, I hang out with Kristin and friends from the salon when he's working. They all think his money talk is stupid too. Now, I'm not saying that money isn't important. But, we're young, and we don't have a house, kids, and those kind of responsibilities yet, so why not enjoy ourselves?

Luke really started to get on my nerves. He is a neat freak for one thing. He wants everything in its place. I'm not a slob, but he is too neat. If the shoes aren't lined up in the closet, he will re-organize them. If the bedspread has a lump in the middle, he'll re-make the bed. I knew he was only doing that to 'show me' I was wrong, because they were my shoes he was lining up, and it was me who made the bed that wasn't perfectly smooth. I would work all day, then come home and clean, but it didn't seem good enough. There were other things too. He hadn't brought me flowers in a long time, and since Kristin told him off, he hadn't brought me lunch either. I missed having lunch with Luke. After listening to all that, Kendall suggested I make him a special dinner and tell him how I was feeling. So I did.

Luke was shocked to see a candle light dinner waiting him when he got home. He hugged me, and gave me one of *his* kisses. I emphasize *his* because they are like no other kiss I've ever had! I made his favorite: grilled shrimp scampi. He thanked me, told me how beautiful I looked, then asked how my day was. I talked about the girls at the salon and their guy troubles. I talked about my clients, and that Meredith is pregnant with her second baby. Why she got pregnant again, when all she does is complain about the baby she already has, is a mystery to me. I talked for awhile before I realized I hadn't asked about his day. He shrugged his shoulders and said, "It was alright."

After dinner, I asked him to come and sit on the couch so we could talk. I told him that I had some things that I needed to tell him, things that had been bothering me lately. I started very calmly. I told him that I missed him, and that I was trying to do better with my spending habits. (I hadn't bought anything new in over a week.) I continued to tell him that I felt that he was disappointed with me, and that I knew he was sending me messages by fixing my

shoes in the closet, re-making the bed, etc.. I continued with my list which detailed more things that annoyed me for about 45 minutes. He didn't say a thing while I talked. He looked at the wall; nodding on occasion. When I was done, he was still looking at the wall. Since his quietness was one of his more annoying qualities, I found myself getting really mad the longer he just sat there not saying anything. Finally, I exploded, "WELL..." Then he looked at me. I saw sadness in his eyes. "It must be very hard for you to live with a person who is so awful," Luke finally replied. Why did he have to say something like that? I didn't say he was awful. I said he was annoying.

What came next felt like a giant slap in the face, though he never touched me. "I'm sorry. I'll try to do better." That was it. That was all he said. He didn't get mad, he didn't say a bunch of stuff about me that annoyed him. He just said he was sorry, then got up and went for a walk. The following Sunday we spent the day at his parents house. I sat with his mom on the patio while we ate lunch. I watched Luke as he threw the Frisbee with Josie, the family's golden retriever. She was fat, old, and limped, but she played Frisbee with Luke like she was a pup. It made me smile.

Lily, Luke's mom, asked me how things were going. Another ally, I thought. I started down my list of complaints, then told her of our dinner and conversation from a few days before. She nodded, looking at her salad, then to Luke, but said nothing. Must be a Walker trait.

Things stayed pretty much the same over the next several months. We had come to some kind of truce, but I wasn't exactly sure what that was. We just existed together: nothing bad, but nothing great. Luke was true to his promise to do better though. He didn't re-make the bed, and he left my shoes in a heap. All this time, Kendall kept listening to me.

One day I was telling Kendall that I thought I was falling out of love with Luke. Things were boring, he wasn't the same guy he was when we were dating, and while he wasn't bad to me, things were stale. I didn't think it was worth staying with him. Then it happened.

Her eyes narrowed at me, and she quietly, but firmly said, "Shut up." I looked stunned at her in the mirror. She stared right back with a look that pierced me.

"What?" I said stupidly.

"You heard me," Kendall replied.

I spun her chair around to look at her properly. "I know what you said, I..." I started to reply but she cut me off.

"You are the most selfish, spoiled, little girl I've ever known." Her tone was flat, soft, yet powerful. I'm sure my mouth was hanging open. Then, as she sat there staring at me, tears started flowing from her eyes with alarming speed. "You have no idea what you will be throwing away. You have a good husband. You haven't tried hard enough to make things better." What...? She had no idea what she was talking about.

"What do you know about it?" I snapped hotly.

"Well, I've listened to you talk about Luke for what, three years now? You used to go on and on about how perfect he is, and now all you do is criticize him, belittle

How will thinking, "It will never happen to us" prevent it from happening to us?

him, talk badly about him. It's no wonder you've fallen out of love with him. Did you ever really love *him* in the first place?"

She said the word "him" with a different tone. I sat down. Who was this woman, and why was she talking to me like this?

"Look," she said. "I'm sorry for being so blunt. But really Rachel, you haven't worked hard enough at your marriage to give it up yet."

"Oh, really?" I quipped back. Did she even have a husband?

She quietly started, "You'll never have a successful marriage if you can't get past all these petty, stupid, little things you are always going on about." She had my full attention. I couldn't take my eyes off her face. The tears were still rolling. "I realize that no man is perfect," she went on, "but neither are we. Has Luke ever listed your faults to you in the way you've done to him?" That stung, because I knew he hadn't.

"I have a funeral to attend tomorrow." Her statement caught me off guard. It had nothing to do with what she had just been saying.

"You mentioned that when you came in," was my response.

"It's my husband's funeral." Her voice was almost a whisper. My eyes widened. "He'd been fighting cancer

12 Ounce of Prevention   HealthyMarriageTips.com

for about four years now."

How could I not know this? I had seen her every few weeks for three years. Truth is, I never asked anything about her, and she never volunteered any information. I always started in with my own problems.

"Bart and I have been married for 25 years. I was young when he swept me off my feet." Her face calmed as she reminisced. She was silent before continuing. "He was everything a girl could want: kind, gentle, a hard worker... much like your Luke. But there was always a quiet side that he wouldn't share. It bothered me a lot. Just like Luke's quietness bothers you." No wonder she seemed to understand me, she had been there. "One day, after being married for a few years, I talked to my mom. I cried, and wondered why Bart had been so wonderful, then had become someone I could hardly stand to be around. My mom sat me up, and looked me straight in the eye with a look I'd never seen before; she was really mad." Kendall sat up in her chair, in demonstrative fashion.

"Kendall Jean Robbins," she announced with a strong southern accent, "you hush your mouth right now. Bart is not a perfect man, and if you thought so, you were mistakin.'" I couldn't help smiling at Kendall; I almost laughed outright. "But," Kendall continued in a motherish voice, "he is a good man, with good qualities and that's why you fell in love with him. You're spending so much time concerned with the little things he does that bother you. Have you considered the things you're doin' that bother him?" Kendall let out a chuckle as she recalled her mother. "You stop lookin' for the bad in that man, and start lookin' for the good. You speak well of him in front of others, and start treatin' him like you did while you were courtin'. You do that, and he'll look like he did back then, only better."

If you can control your tone of voice when the phone rings why can't you do the same for your spouse?

"Better?" I questioned.

"Yes," Kendall said with a sly smile, before sliding into the accent again, "'Cause now you two ain't just courtin,' you're married, and bein' married has a few more advantages!" We both let out a laugh, lessening the tension. "But even with advantages, love and marriage takes work. More work than you've been putting in." Kendall sat back.

"She was right, Rachel." Kendall got serious again, her cheeks glistening, "Bart was nowhere near perfect, and neither am I. But I took her advice, and it changed *everything*. I started remembering his good qualities, and along the way I discovered new things that made me love him even more. As I started changing the way I acted toward him, he suddenly became the man I fell in love with…only better! I realized I wasn't giving him much of a reason to want to be with me, because of the way I was treating him." Her eyes were pleading with me to understand. "But things were better when we both worked at it. When we found out he had cancer, I was devastated. I love my husband deeply; I didn't want him to suffer. I didn't want him to die." I was choking up now. Kendall said in a pleading whisper, "You need to remember why you fell in love with Luke. Honestly Rach, are shoes, the bed, and all those other little complaints *worth it*? Look at how they have changed the way you feel about Luke."

I felt a stab of shame as her words landed right where they were meant to land. My heart beat heavily as I considered it all. As I replayed the past two years in my mind, I saw she was right. I hugged Kendall tightly. "I'm so sorry about Bart," I managed to choke out.

"Thank you," she whispered. "Just don't give up. Marriage is a life long journey, not a destination. It will take both of you, together, to make it work." I finished her hair in silence.

Luke came with me to Bart Robbin's funeral. As I listened to the family speak about Bart and Kendall, their deep love for each other, their strong marriage, I knew that I wanted-- no-- I needed, a marriage like that. I turned and looked at Luke with tears in my eyes. We both had said and done things that damaged our relationship. But, with Kendall's words fresh in my mind, I was determined to make our marriage better.

We stayed up all night talking after the funeral. I apologized to Luke for my part in creating the tension in our marriage. Luke hugged me fiercely; I didn't want him to let go. He apologized for his part in the tensions too. I told him what I needed from him, and he told me what he needed from me. Together, we recommitted ourselves to our marriage and to each other. He started opening up and talking more; I complained less and listened more. We started making the bed together. We ate by candle light more, like tonight. It's our third anniversary; and you know, I'm more in love with Luke now than on our wedding day. I'm still Kendall's hair stylist, but now I do a lot more listening.

Ounce of Prevention Worksheet

Do you ever find yourself dwelling on your spouses faults?

The more you dwell on your spouse's faults, the more faults you will find. As you find more faults, your respect for your spouse decreases and feelings of contempt will increase. The longer you allow this cycle to continue, the greater the damage to your marriage will occur.

The reality is that everyone has faults, including yourself. Even if you divorce your spouse, you will end up simply trading in one set of faults for a different set of faults in your next relationship. The key to a happy marriage is to learn to live with your spouse just the way they are and not dwell on their faults.

This week, if you notice a fault of your spouse's, immediately write down five qualities that you admire about your spouse. Begin this exercise right now by writing down four positive qualities.

1.

2.

3.

4.

As you dwell on your spouse's strengths, the respect you feel towards your spouse will increase, contempt will decrease, and you will enjoy the fruits of a happy and healthy marriage.

There are some faults that should never be tolerated. Domestic violence is one of them. If you are the victim of domestic violence, please contact a professional immediately.

Growing a Marriage Garden

That had been the happiest day of her life she thought bitterly as she looked at the wedding picture. She and Peter looked so happy in the picture, so excited to begin their lives together and share the bliss that was marriage. Unfortunately, their happiness had gone downhill from there. Peter had left after their last screaming match and probably wouldn't be home for at least an hour.

Beth sighed and went outside to water her plants. They were the one bright spot in her life. As she filled the watering can, she mentally reviewed the fight. She couldn't easily identify the spark that had ignited it. Over the past two years of their marriage, they had engaged in increasingly regular shouted battles. There were so few things she remembered about why she fell in love with Peter in the first place. Though she and Peter dated for two years and had a six-month engagement, she now felt like she didn't know him. She thought she had known him as much as anyone did and loved him, so they got married.

Beth started soaking her precious flowers carefully and started a conversation with her petunias about her husband.

"He is so self-centered," she muttered. "He doesn't even seem to notice how hard I work to save money. He only notices to complain when I spend more than a few dollars, even though he regularly buys frivolous things." Beth continued to mumble aloud her husband-related frustrations, getting increasingly heated.

"Good afternoon." The intrusion of a human voice startled Beth out of her disgruntled musings. She looked behind her to see her neighbor peeking over the fence and blushed deeply.

"Sorry for startling you, but I couldn't help hearing what you were saying while I was weeding, and I didn't want to overhear something I shouldn't," Beth's neighbor said with a smile.

"Oh, it's okay, Jane," Beth replied wryly. "I shouldn't be talking to myself anyway."

"Sometimes thoughts and feelings just need to be expressed," Jane said. "I find that I talk to myself more often than I would like to admit."

"Sorry to bother you." Beth started to turn back to her flowers when Jane stopped her.

"Oh, it's okay. I was about ready to take a break anyway and check on Emma. Hey, I've got some cold lemonade. Why don't you come over and we'll have some."

Beth hesitated, feeling the need to be with her plants to work out her frustrations. She opened her mouth to decline the invitation, but found herself accepting. Still wondering why she was going to visit with her neighbor, Beth went through the gate and followed Jane into her kitchen.

"Just have a seat and I'll get that lemonade." Jane set down the baby monitor and started opening her cupboards to get glasses out while Beth sat down at the kitchen table. The phone rang and Jane picked it up. Beth couldn't help but hear half of the conversation.

"Hello…How's my handsome husband? …Good. I've just been weeding and invited Beth over for some

What is one weakness that you have that has a negative impact on your marriage and how can you turn it into a strength?

lemonade. How is work going? ...Good....Okay. I love you too."

"What did Jim want?" Beth asked when Jane ended the phone call.

"Nothing in particular. He calls me everyday just to say hi." Jane smiled and brought the lemonade over to the table.

"Really?" Beth asked incredulously. "Every day?"

"We miss a few here and there, but almost every day," Jane replied, still smiling. "It brightens my day and his, and helps us stay connected and in love."

"You seem to really love your husband. How long have you been married?"

"We have been married for five of the best years of my life."

"Wow," Beth said softly. Jane looked at her with concern, and a wrinkle appeared on her forehead. She opened her mouth, hesitated, and then released her breath. She paused again, then seemed to gather up her courage.

"Beth, I couldn't help overhearing a few of your comments while you were watering," Jane started gently. "I don't mean to intrude but is everything okay between you and Peter?" When Beth didn't respond, Jane continued. "Every couple has disagreements; we're all human. But I get the feeling that you aren't very happy in your marriage. Is there anything you want to talk about? I'm told I'm a

20 Ounce of Prevention   HealthyMarriageTips.com

pretty good listener." The silence stretched out, then tears started to well in Beth's eyes.

"I have to talk to someone," she blurted out. "Whenever I say anything to Peter about what he is doing that bothers me, he just yells back at me." Jane reached over to the kitchen counter to get some tissues and silently handed one to Beth. "He is such a frustrating, self-centered egotist. He thinks that everything he does is perfect and that I am worth nothing. He never asks my opinion on anything or takes me out anymore. He treats me like a door mat. We keep fighting more and more about everything. We have such different ideas that we never should have gotten married. His family is so irksome and frustrating, and he defends them. He never sees that something might be different from the way he does things." With every sentence, Beth grew more upset and her voice slowly got louder. The baby monitor on the kitchen counter lit up, and a few whimpers interrupted Beth's tirade. "Oh, Jane, I'm so sorry I forgot about your baby sleeping," Beth said in a softer voice, "I should go."

"Nonsense, it's about time for her to be up anyway," Jane replied. "If you promise not to go anywhere, I'll go get her." Beth promised, and Jane soon returned with a sleepy eight-month-old.

"I'm sorry I woke her up," Beth began apologizing again. "I didn't mean to get so loud or burden you with my struggles."

"Don't worry about it," Jane said. "She normally gets up about this time anyway." Jane made a face at Emma who smiled and rubbed the sleep out of her eyes. "See, she's fine."

After watching Jane interact with Emma for a few minutes, Beth hesitatingly asked, "Is she why you and Jim are so happy?" Jane looked up surprised, and then

What would you do differently if you found out that your spouse had only weeks to live?

her glance softened with understanding.

"Yes and no," she replied. "Yes, she definitely contributes to our overall happiness, though at times she tries our patience considerably. However, Jim and I were happy before we had her. He is a wonderful man, and we love being with each other."

"Maybe I just picked the wrong man," Beth said almost to herself.

"Oh, I don't think so," Jane said. "I watched you when you first moved in; you were both so happy and in love."

"Well, we fight more than we enjoy each other's company now. Something isn't working out." Beth sighed and put her forehead in her hand. "We've even contemplated divorce, though neither of us wants to admit we've failed at marriage."

"I don't think it's nearly time to call it quits," Jane protested. "Every marriage has a few problems, but they can be fixed."

"You don't have problems."

"Yes, we do," Jane chuckled. "We just work hard to make our marriage happy by working through our problems."

"How am I supposed to do that?" Beth asked. "I don't even know what the problem is. The only thing I can think of is that I don't really love him anymore." She grabbed another tissue and stared at the table, ready to catch her tears as they rolled down her cheeks.

"Watching you now," Jane said softly, "I'm pretty sure you still love him."

"What good is that going to do me if all I keep doing is learning how to hate him!" Beth protested.

Jane put Emma on the floor with a teething ring and gently put her hand over Beth's. "There are many things that you can do to improve your marriage. One of the things that has helped Jim and me have a happy marriage is to talk out our differences."

"But when I do that, the only thing that happens is a big fight," Beth countered.

"I'm talking about communication, not arguing. Talking through differences doesn't mean you have to raise your voices or yell at each other. When Jim and I get into an argument, we don't accomplish anything except hurt feelings until we calm down and discuss the problem evenly, without raised voices. Occasionally we let things get too heated, and we need a cooling off period away from each other before we can discuss the problem." Jane paused and Beth looked up.

"We do that," Beth began. "We fight, then take a break but if we go back to the subject we just start fighting again, so I've stopped bringing up painful subjects. Unfortunately, everything from money to family get-togethers has become a painful subject." Beth dabbed her eyes and continued, "We don't talk anymore except to fight. There don't seem to be any happy subjects to discuss. Everything he does bothers me." Jane squeezed Beth's hand in sympathy then took a careful breath.

"I got into a situation similar to that with Jim once. I just had to remind myself that I loved him and resolve to talk over our differences calmly. There are a lot of moments

You would never cling to a hot rock so why is it so hard to let go of anger?

even during the discussion that I had to pause, take a deep breath, and count to ten to keep my cool. As silly as counting to ten may sound, it's worked for me."

"But I just feel like I dislike Peter even more after every argument. How can I go back and try to discuss something with him if I'm having trouble loving him anymore?"

"Well, it sounds like you need to rekindle your love. When Jim and I are going through a rough patch, or I find myself getting complacent in my love for him, I do something special for him to show him and myself I really do love him." A slobbery teething ring skittered across the floor accompanied by a shriek from Emma demanding its return. Jane smiled, retrieved the toy and went to the sink to rinse it off. "She really knows how to interrupt important conversations."

The corners of Beth's mouth twitched up for a moment. "What are some of the things you do?"

"Oh, anything and everything," Jane said as she returned the clean toy to Emma and sat back at the table. "I've made a romantic candlelight dinner for him with his favorite dish; I've made lists of reasons why I love him, both to remind me and later to give to him." Jane refilled their lemonade glasses and continued. "I think the most important thing to keep in mind while you're doing something is you need to either open lines of communication or keep open those you have. Constant, open, loving communication is the only reason Jim and I have been able to remain happy and keep our marriage intact." Jane interrupted herself to snatch a dried leaf away from Emma just as she was about to put it in her mouth. As Jane put Emma in her high chair with a snack, Beth thought about what had been said. She felt a glimmer of hope that maybe her marriage wasn't destined for failure. It might just work out if she and Peter could learn how to speak kindly to each other. Looking back over the time they dated, she realized that they hadn't had too many serious discussions about life or their goals. Afraid she might get discouraged, she looked up at Jane.

"I don't think Peter and I really know how to communicate. Do you think we could learn?" Beth asked hope flickering in her eyes.

"Everyone can learn how to communicate. It can take a lot of effort; it can take a lot of willpower, but it can be done." Jane looked at the resolve entering Beth's eyes and posture and continued. "From what you've told me, both you and Peter want this marriage to work. I think if you talk to him softly about things and refrain from any blame-placing or name-calling, you might be surprised at the results." As Beth sat quietly absorbing what Jane had said, she seemed to come to a decision.

"I think I'll give it a shot," she decided aloud.

"Good for you," Jane encouraged. "If there is any support or help I can give, let me know."

"Actually," Beth hesitated, "I'm not sure I know how to just talk about something without sparking an argument."

"Well, just as much as it takes two people to fight it also takes two people cooperating to discuss something. But," Jane countered, "there are some things that you can

Why are we willing to invest so much time and money into our wedding yet are reluctant to invest time and money into helping our marriage last a lifetime?

do to try and facilitate a discussion."

"What?" Beth asked.

"First of all, make sure that you remain calm and don't get upset at something Peter says. Also, try to avoid verbally attacking him. It will put him on the defensive and you won't be able to get as much done." Jane smiled encouragingly. "The best person to talk with about your marital difficulties is your husband because he is the only one who can fix anything." Beth was starting to look a little overwhelmed, so Jane hurried to continue. "No attempt will be perfect. Even if there are a few setbacks, stay motivated; things will get better."

"Well, I'd better be getting back home and make something for dinner." Beth pushed back her chair and stood up. "Thanks for giving me advice," she said awkwardly.

"What are friends for," Jane replied. She stood up and hugged Beth. "If you ever need someone to motivate you to keep working on your marriage, I'm here."

"Thanks," Beth said and smiled. "You've given me hope that my marriage isn't over." After goodbyes were said, Beth crossed back over into her yard and walked up the steps to her door. She saw Peter's car was back and took a deep breath. She pushed open the door and saw Peter sitting dejectedly on the couch.

"Hi," Beth said softly.

"I'm done," Peter replied. "I can't take all this fighting anymore."

"Are you saying you want out of the marriage?" Beth asked, fear entering her heart.

"I guess," Peter said. "We've failed, haven't we? Isn't that what you want?"

"No," Beth said, and continued with growing conviction. "I don't want out. I want to give our marriage another try. I think we can make it work if we're willing to give it another shot." She paused as Peter looked up at her. She took a deep breath and continued, "I realized today I still love you and want to make this marriage work." The silence stretched out and a look of astonishment appeared on Peter's face.

"You still love me?" Peter questioned softly.

"Yes."

"But what about all our differences and all the fights we have?" Peter countered. "Do you really think this marriage can work?"

"I don't know, but I'd like to try. It's going to take a lot of work." Beth looked at him. "I know we fight a lot, but we don't ever really resolve any of our differences. You…" Beth stopped, remembered what Jane had said about not attacking, and tried to rethink what she would say. "I know I have faults and need to work harder at this marriage, but I need help from you too." Beth took a tentative step toward Peter. "I'd like to learn how to talk with you not just fight with you. Would you be willing to give our marriage another try?"

"Yeah," Peter slowly replied. "Let's work on it." He looked at Beth with an emotion showing in his eyes she hadn't seen for a while. "I think I still love you too."

Beth set the freshly dusted picture back on the shelf

Why are we so willing to spend time and energy planning for a vacation yet are reluctant to create a plan to strengthen our marriage?

next to the other pictures. She smiled as she thought of the occasion for the picture. She and Peter had gone on a vacation to celebrate their fourth wedding anniversary. With how happy she was now, it was sometimes hard to remember that just over two years ago her marriage had been on the verge of disintegration. Peter had agreed to give their marriage another try, and they had worked hard on keeping their communication open and healthy. They had struggled with being able to stay calm during discussions and had consulted a marriage counselor. After awhile they were able to communicate their hopes and dreams as well as calmly discuss their differences. They still had differences, and occasionally their discussions became heated, but overall their communication had improved immensely. Their marriage was healthy and strong, and they were both happier than they had ever been.

    Beth heard the timer go off, and she hurried to pull Peter's favorite dinner from the oven. As she put the finishing touches on the table, she heard his car pull up. She was lighting the candles as a bouquet of flowers preceded her husband through the door. He stopped short at the sight of the candlelight dinner she had prepared and then smiled.

    "I love you, Beth."
    "I love you too, Peter."

Ounce of Prevention Worksheet

In the beginning of each of our relationships we start out with a beautiful marriage garden. The flowers smell sweet and love is definitely in the air. If a weed appears, we immediately get rid of it. It seems as if the garden just flourishes on its own with little, if any, effort on our part.

In reality the garden is flourishing because of all the time and effort we spend nurturing our relationship, combined with a heavy dose of hormones. As time goes by, we find that the neglected areas of our lives scream for our time and attention. Slowly our efforts in our marriage gardens begin to drop off.

Weeds appear, flowers no longer bloom as magnificently, the sweet aroma of love seems to have dissipated and many are left to wonder if they made a mistake or if the garden was ever as magnificent as they remembered. Even worse is when they imagine they could create a better garden with someone else.

The truth is, if you want a lifelong beautiful marriage garden, it is going to take consistent time and effort on your part to grow and maintain it. The easy times you remember in the beginning of the relationship were actually due to a drug induced euphoria that our bodies produced to help us fall in love. The hormones that created this state diminish over time and are usually no longer being produced as intensely within 1-2 years. However, you can still experience that intense natural high with your spouse, but you have to put the time and effort in to release the hormones in higher quantities.

It is far easier to grow and maintain a garden if you spend

time each day caring for it. If you wait too long the weeds will seem to have overgrown the garden and the task of restoring the garden to its former beauty may seem too overwhelming. Almost any couple can successfully restore their garden and create it even more magnificent than ever before. But this takes consistent TIME and EFFORT.

The best time to start taking care of your marriage garden is now. Plant some small flowers by doing small acts of kindness for your spouse. Water the soil by expressing your appreciation for what your spouse has done for you today or in the past. Pull some weeds by forgiving your spouse for things that have been said or done recently. The most critical thing you can do is look at your marriage garden and find the areas where you have deposited the poison of selfishness. Nothing will kill a marriage garden faster than the toxic poison called selfishness. The antidote to selfishness is service, so replace those areas with a healthy dose of service.

A lifelong beautiful marriage garden doesn't just happen on its own. If you want it, MAKE IT HAPPEN. Don't wait for your spouse to start helping. Eventually he or she will join you in your efforts. Be patient, get started and you will start to experience the fruits of your efforts.

Make a list of the specific things you will do this week to spend time and effort growing and maintaining your marriage garden.

What is one weakness that you have that has a negative impact on your marriage and how can you turn it into a strength?

Creating a Soul Mate

He was perfect: my prince Charming. I was a terrible romantic when I met him, and I gave up my heart the day he smiled at me. I know, what a sap. Still, to my credit, he was very dashing. The first time I saw him was at one of those fancy dances at the university, where he was dressed in a long tailed tuxedo. His vest and tie were a deep burgundy, and his skin was dark like brown sugar with his black hair combed carefully into casual waves over his forehead. His cheeks were high and broad and his jaw was strong. He was my date's friend, and he introduced him to me. That was when he smiled at me. The smile spread across his whole face and lit his eyes so they turned to golden honey.

We danced once that night. I can't remember anything else that happened after we did. All I can remember is the electrifying sensation of his one hand at my waist and the other holding mine gently. I didn't see him again for an agonizing two months. Then, fate or destiny brought us together.

We were in the same ballroom class. It was perfect; I got to see him every day for an hour. My semester revolved around that class and my chance to dance with him. He asked me to be his testing partner for the first midterm, and after that we practiced habitually. After our last performance in Spring, he asked me to marry him.

After a year, I found myself wondering what went wrong. If he was Mr. Perfect, then why was I unhappy? I still loved him. My heart ached to think of us apart, but when he was near, I was annoyed. So, it was not without relief I left him for two weeks to visit my family. It took a month to convince him to let me go.

"You know," I said, "both my mother and my brother are graduating next month."

"Yes," he said without looking up from his dinner. When I didn't say anything, he glanced at my face. "Yes, I wish we could go. Unfortunately, I have to work."

"I think it is very important that I go, John."

"I know, Jen. I'm sorry; it's just that it will be impossible for me to take that much time off. Besides, you know we can't spare the money."

"I can work extra hours this month to make up for lost time," I murmured, pushing peas around my plate.

"Jen," his voice was pleading. "We've been through this before. I don't want you to work anymore than you have to."

"My father has offered to pay for the flight."

He sighed. "Jen, I can't go."

I suddenly felt unexplainably angry. Words came unbidden to my throat. A soft voice in my head warned me not to act rashly. I opened my mouth to say okay, but the other words were already there.

"You're being selfish. You just don't want me to go." My voice escalated until the last word was a shout. The intensity of my own emotions startled me, and I was immediately ashamed. Then the hurt on his face registered in my brain, and I felt mad and disgusted with myself. I left the table and fled to our room as much in shame as in anger.

When an argument ends would you rather be right or married?

I cried myself to sleep that night and only woke up when John slid in beside me. He enfolded me in his embrace and whispered in my ear.

"I'm sorry," he said. "If you want to go home by yourself, I won't stop you."

My heart melted and I started crying again. I twisted so that I could bury my face in his chest. "I'm sorry, John. It wasn't fair of me to say what I did. You've never been selfish towards me. Please forgive me."

He tightened his arms and kissed the top of my head.

Those weeks before I left were hard. Every time I looked at him I remembered what I'd said, and I was filled with the same conflicting emotions. I began to notice more of his faults. After dinner, he would sit at the table and watch as I washed the dishes. He never once offered to help. If I was too tired to do them, they collected in the sink. When I complained about something, he never sympathized. He wasn't silent either; he berated. I started to feel that anything I told him was a plea for his wisdom. Then, on top of that, he didn't fill up the car until the needle was past empty and he chewed with his mouth open.

I became desperate for the day I could leave and spend two whole weeks away from him. The minute I stepped on the jet plane, relief and happiness flooded through me, but that immediately countered with guilt.

Still, the guilt was not strong enough to stay for very long. I walked out of the terminal and into the arms of mother only two and a half hours later. With her arms around me, I felt a sense of peace and joy I hadn't felt since the day I married John; it brought tears to my eyes.

A few days after her graduation, my mother brought up my marriage. She was cooking dinner and I was sitting at the kitchen bar with my chin in my hands. I hadn't said anything about my marriage, yet somehow she knew everything was not all right. She had always known when I was upset about something.

"You're not happy with John, are you?" She chopped onions while she waited for my reply.

"It's not that I'm not happy with him…I mean, I still love him…it's just that…well…" I trailed off, hopelessly. I tried again. "Mom, do you believe in soul mates?"

"Yes. Your father and I are soul mates."

"Yeah, I know. It's just that I'm not sure anymore that John is my soul mate."

"Nonsense, of course he is your soul mate. You are married, aren't you?" She moved on to the potatoes.

"But what if I made the wrong choice?" I picked up a leaf of lettuce and began to shred it.

My mother stopped chopping and looked up into my eyes. "Jennifer, you would have problems no matter who you chose. 'Happily ever after' does not mean 'carefree ever after.' You made your choice, now you make it the right one."

I picked up another lettuce piece. She had always spoken like that. I guess that's what comes of having a writer for a mother. The problem was that it took awhile to digest what she had said. I was on my fifth lettuce leaf before I had my thoughts organized.

Why can we negotiate a business deal with a stranger but find it so difficult to negotiate financial matters with our spouse?

"Okay, Mom, suppose I did make the right choice. Why does he annoy me then?"

"Why does he annoy you?"

I told her everything I could think of. I even told her the way he breathed at night irritated me. I finished with a summary of our conversation the night he told me I could go.

"Oh honey, he really loves you. He loves you so much he can't bear the thought of you getting hurt because he wasn't there to protect you."

"But I'm an adult, mom. I can take care of myself. I don't need constant supervision. That's why I moved out of here."

"I know you can take care of yourself. But you must keep in mind that men feel protective of the things they love. More importantly, you must remember that marriage is a bonding relationship. This means he is responsible for your well-being just as you are responsible for his. Marriage means you have accepted him into your life. You and he are one person; damage to one is damage to the other as well."

"That doesn't change my irritation. I often feel annoyed with myself."

"Then I suggest that you first forgive yourself and then try to emphasize his good qualities. When he does something that bothers you, counter it with the reasons you love him. Also, think of what you have in common and expand them. Play new games, watch new movies, read books together, try new things so you can have more in common. You should have one night a week when you go dancing together, or something like it that you both like to do."

We were both silent after this. It all sounded so churchish. I couldn't imagine how it could possibly work. I reached for another piece.

"Jen, I was hoping to make a green salad with that. As it is, we're going to have a salad of barely identifiable lettuce. If you want to help, you can set the table."

The next day, my mother helped me start the 'Superman Program,' as she called it. The goal was to make him out to be even better than Superman. It was a bit embarrassing, really.

"You say he chews with his mouth open, right?"

I nodded.

"Okay, but he does have a strong jaw, doesn't he?"

I giggled. "Yes, mom, he has a very strong jaw." I remembered the feel of his jaw under my hands and the way the muscles rippled when he clenched his teeth.

"Good, now what about the shape of his mouth?"

I chuckled again. "Very shapely. I can't imagine a better shaped mouth for kissing."

"Or for eating." We both laughed.

"And he has perfect teeth."

"Yes, he does, and now you can see them even when he eats."

That was how it began. It was actually really fun. Then something happened and I stopped commenting on just his physical attributes. I started thinking about his character. It wasn't long before I missed some of the things that used to annoy me. I really, truly missed him. I

> Why are we willing to take our car in for an oil change every 3000 miles, yet never find time for a tune-up for our marriage?

couldn't wait to get home because now home was wherever John was.

The airport was a good hour away from our house, and my flight was during the day. I knew John had to work, and I was planning on taking the shuttle like I had on the way in. But when I got to the baggage claim, he was there with his beautiful smile and a welcome kiss. I didn't even mind that he was wearing sandals despite the rain. After all, he did have nice feet.

Ounce of Prevention Worksheet

They say that love is blind, which is apparent when you look at any couple falling in love. As we start to fall in love we tend to either ignore the other person's faults, or we put a positive spin on their faults. So if our friends say he is cheap, we say he is thrifty. If they say he is a know-it-all we inform them he is a renaissance man. What makes the problem even worse is we both tend to hide our own faults as well.

After we get married, we let our guard down and are more willing to allow our spouse to discover some of the faults we've been hiding. At about the same time the rose colored glasses that helped our spouse put a positive spin on our faults tend to come off. In the end, we are both left thinking that we have been deceived.

No one is perfect, and everyone brings their own set of faults to their marriage. Unfortunately, many people become disillusioned at this point, get a divorce and set off looking for their "true soul mate." Those who choose this course are met with disappointment after disappointment until they discover the truth that a soul mate does not mean a perfect mate, and that a soul mate relationship is CREATED, not found.

One step to creating a soul mate relationship is to develop the habit of playing the Create a Soul Mate game.

The first step is to look for your spouse's strengths and remind yourself of them on a daily basis.

The second step is to rediscover the skill you possessed

when you were falling in love. Learn to put a positive spin on his or her faults. Constantly noticing his or her faults and pointing them out is simply not going to turn those faults into strengths. It's far better to use that energy to get used to your spouse rather than constantly trying to change him or her.

The sooner we are able to learn to love our spouse with all their weaknesses, the sooner we will be able to start enjoying years of living in a healthy and happy marriage.

There are some faults that should never be tolerated. Domestic violence is one of them. If you are a victim of domestic violence please, seek professional help immediately.

> Why do we allow pride to create so much damage to our marriage?

What's in a Name
By Dan Hope

The Hendersons were a happy couple.

But by no means were they perfect. Brad refused to watch *What Not to Wear*. Melanie hated *SportsCenter*. Brad constantly forgot to take out the garbage. Melanie would frequently leave her makeup all over the vanity. Brad forgot the exact date of the first time they kissed. Melanie couldn't care less about Kobe Bryant's shooting record.

But despite all the things that didn't match up, Brad and Melanie did. They had learned how to give and take, and they were happy together, albeit not in front of the same TV.

That's why it was such a shock to find a disagreement they just couldn't handle.

Brad and Melanie were very excited to have children. When Melanie started to suspect she was pregnant, they rushed to the grocery store to buy pregnancy tests. Brad felt mildly embarrassed that it was the only thing they were buying. He could almost hear the cashier thinking, "So what have you guys been up to?" But soon it was over and they were back at home, huddled over a little stick with a window that may or may not have contained a plus. After arguing for several minutes over what shade the vertical bar had to achieve to actually constitute a plus, not a minus, they finally agreed they were pregnant. After a long hug and some nervous, but happy, giggles they settled down and let reality sink in.

"You know what this means?" Melanie asked.

Brad's head was suddenly full of shopping lists. Bottles, diapers, and doctor's bills floated through his head, all bearing enormous, red dollar signs. "I'll need to get a second job?"

"What? No. I mean we need to pick a name."

"Oh," Brad said, quite relieved. "That part's easy. We're just going to name him after my great-grandfather."

Melanie was immediately indignant he had picked a name without even consulting her. After all, she was the mother. To make matters worse, she was always suspicious of names dating back more than one generation. "There are two problems with that idea. First, you haven't consulted me, and second, we don't even know if it will be a boy.

Brad was puzzled. "I thought the first kid in every family was a boy." Melanie stared in disbelief. "Isn't it?" he said, suddenly uncomfortable under his wife's incredulous gaze. He had the distinct feeling he might have said something wrong. Unfortunately, male intuition is vastly different than female intuition, in that men don't get any warnings until *after* the damage is done.

"Brad, I'm the oldest child in my family."

"Right," he said quickly. Then he thought about it. "Ohhhh."

"Look, whether it's a boy or a girl, we need to do this together. So let's just be civilized about this. Ok, what's your great-grandfather's name?"

"You're going to love it. His name was Delbert."

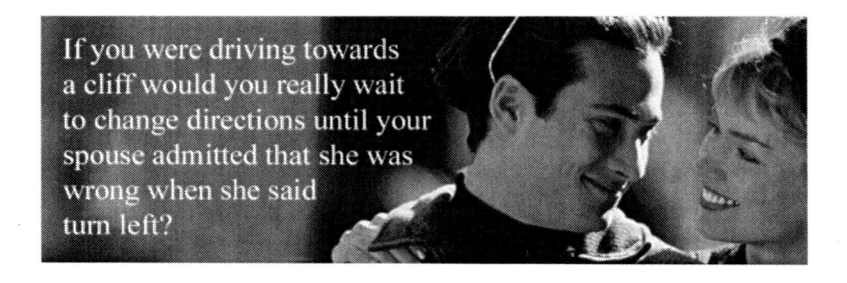

> If you were driving towards a cliff would you really wait to change directions until your spouse admitted that she was wrong when she said turn left?

Melanie nearly swallowed her tongue in surprise. She immediately forgot about civility.

"You want to name our child Delbert!" she cried. "I can't think of a more idiotic name. You're practically dooming him to constant bullying."

"C'mon now," Brad said, a little peeved. His ancestors were most certainly not idiotic. "We won't call him Delbert all the time. We can call him Del."

"Like the farmer in the dell? Like Dell Computers? No matter which way you look at it, he's doomed to dorkdom."

"Ok hotshot, what've you got?"

Melanie smiled. What more perfect way to calm the argument than with the name that was undeniably perfect. "Well, we don't actually have to worry about whether it's a boy or girl because I have the best name for both. We'll name our baby Leslie."

Brad almost fainted. "You'll give my boy a girl's name? Why don't you just put a dress on him and paint his nails! And I'm not paying for ballet lessons; let's just get that straight right now."

The Hendersons were not a happy couple.

That night turned out to be a long one. As soon as Melanie heard the name Delbert, she had sensed this could turn into a big conflict. As was mentioned, female intuition is vastly superior to male intuition because it comes before the storm. Unfortunately, most women are to sure they are right and just head into the wind anyway. Intuition is like an appendix: nobody uses it.

Melanie was worried because she never thought they would disagree on something so simple as a name. Brad was still mad about having an "idiotic" great-grandpa.

They spent the next few days avoiding the topic of names. But that also meant they never talked about the baby. Eventually it became too much for them, and they softened a little. They hugged. They apologized. They laughed at how stupid they had been. They promised to be a team, to make a joint decision.

"You know, I'm not even that big on Delbert anymore," Brad said, enjoying the feeling of being close to Melanie. He'd spent the last few days being politely but firmly kept at arms length.

"That's good, because I never was," Melanie said.

"So what now?"

"Well, we won't go into this thinking we have the answer," she said, smiling ruefully. "We'll just throw names out there and start narrowing them down."

"Ok. I've been thinking and I've got a few good ones. How about Haner?" Melanie just looked at him. "Oh c'mon Mel, it's a masculine name."

"Because it sounds like an underwear company?"

"What? It's just, kinda…you know." Brad tried a growl to see if that would make it sound any more masculine.

It just made Melanie cringe. She tried to restrain herself. She was going to be the adult here, even if it gave her an aneurysm. "Ok…that's one option."

Brad seemed to take encouragement from the fact that she didn't dismiss it outright. "How about this one? I thought you might like this because we can use it for a boy

> Why are we willing to spend so much time and money on our hair, nails, skin, etc. but are reluctant to use time and money learning the skills to improve our marriage?

or a girl. We'll call our baby Amsterdam."

Melanie decided to walk away before she did something that might harm the baby.

The Hendersons were still not a happy couple.

They eventually came to the decision they would stick to more common names. This made Melanie a little less anxious and gave Brad a way to focus. They started a list where they couldn't cross names off; they could only circle the ones they liked. It quickly became apparent that none of the names had been circled twice. And there were definitely a few names that begged to be crossed out.

Brad didn't like the name Mary because he had a crazy Aunt Mary. Melanie didn't want a child named Amy because a cheerleader in her high school named that had always made fun of her. Brad didn't want a son named Michael because he knew a geek with that name. Melanie's old boss was named Brian, so that was out of the question. They both started to like the name Megan, until it was revealed that Brad once had a girlfriend by that name. That was the point where the list got torn up.

The Hendersons were really not a happy couple.

They knew they still loved each other. They knew they

loved the baby. They just couldn't figure out why this was such a big problem. Melanie was nearly half way through her pregnancy, and all the changes in her body were making her uncomfortable. The mood swings and cravings were leaving Brad uncomfortable, and it was even worse when Melanie had them too.

Brad was disappointed. He wanted a boy, but they were having a girl. He couldn't even come up with any good girl's names. He had started dismissing each of Melanie's names, not because he disliked them, but as a retaliation for being turned down so often.

They hadn't talked about names for weeks. They had both reached a point where peace was more important than a name. But as the due date neared, they knew a decision was inevitable. When they would thumb through a magazine or a book, their eyes would stop at each name, silently agonizing over whether their daughter would be named Sandra, or Andrea, or Allison, or Apple Blossom. They were beginning to scrape the bottom of the name barrel.

One day Melanie flipped through her family photo album. She came across a picture of her sitting on her grandma's lap. Brad asked, "Who's that?" He immediately wished he hadn't because the answer to the question would be a name, and probably one he'd heard.

"This is my grandma. She died when I was three. I don't remember much about her, but my mother always said she was such a strong woman."

"I'll bet she was. She'd have to be to put up with your grandpa," Brad said.

"She was amazing. I hope our daughter grows up to be like her."

Brad couldn't resist. "What was her name?"

Melanie hesitated, knowing what Brad was going to

> Why do we spend so much time and energy trying to change our spouse?

say. "Her name was Olivia."

Brad thought for a moment before turning back to his book. "I don't like it."

The Hendersons were a scared couple.

Melanie's water broke in the middle of the night while they were in bed. Brad was actually grateful for that because when she rolled over to tell him she was in labor, he thought he might have wet the bed.

Brad made a frantic rush for the door, then a frantic return for the overnight bag, then an even more frantic return for his pregnant wife. He stood still, worried he was forgetting something else. After a minute, he remembered the task at hand and rushed out the door once more.

By the time they finished getting a speeding ticket from a very skeptical police officer and made it to the hospital, Melanie was in a lot of pain. Brad wasn't prepared for it. He had never seen this much pain on anyone's face, let alone his wife's.

He immediately forgot all the months of disagreement and focused on trying to fix it. He became more and more frustrated when he couldn't do anything but stand there and watch. He couldn't fix it! It was his job to protect her; he felt it in his bones, and he was about to go crazy. He could only watch as she did the hardest thing she'd ever done. It was the hardest thing he'd ever done.

As he watched her helplessly, he marveled at how strong she was. He was sure he couldn't do it. She tensed up so hard that her arms became strings of tendons. Her face contorted so much that for long moments he couldn't look at her. But he still couldn't stop thinking about what an amazing woman she was.

Time seemed to move in slow motion. But then, suddenly, it was all over. The nurse handed Brad a tiny bundle. He looked down at a little face that was just as squished as his wife's had been only moments ago. He looked back and forth at the two most beautiful women in his life.

"Mel."

"Yeah, honey," Melanie said, too exhausted to lift her head.

"I love you."

Melanie smiled. She didn't reply because she didn't have to. He knew. He looked back down at his newborn daughter. He knew she would grow up to be a strong woman, just like her mother.

"And I love you, Olivia."

The Hendersons were a happy family.

Ounce of Prevention Worksheet

In math we learn that 2+2=4. In marriage we learn that 1 man + 1 woman sometimes = a disagreement. Disagreements in marriage are inevitable. What is not inevitable is how we choose to handle the disagreements. Unfortunately, most disagreements are handled in ways that damage our relationship. However, it is also possible to learn to handle disagreements in ways that strengthen our relationship. To do so we need to follow a few simple guidelines.

1. Never have a disagreement when one or both of you are upset. Researchers have found when your heart rate climbs 10% above its normal resting rate, you are no longer in control of the rational portion of your brain. This explains why you later regret things you say when you are upset. While it is true you can sometimes resolve a disagreement while you are both upset, you have to ask yourself the question, "At what cost?" Instead of continuing the heated disagreement, CALL A TIMEOUT. Set a time when you will continue the discussion after both of you have calmed down. When you are calm, you are more likely to use the rational part of your brain to solve the problem in a way that can strengthen your marriage.
2. Before you discuss possible solutions, make sure both of you completely understand the other person's position.
3. Be willing to compromise. Many times you will find the compromise is actually better than the solution you wanted. A common barrier to compromise is pride. Beware of pride. Sometimes our pride will blind us to seeing the better solution.
4. Don't discuss a disagreement when you are tired or hungry. Everyone has been told, "Never go to bed

angry." This is actually good advice if you implement it by taking a timeout from the disagreement and agreeing to continue the discussion the following day. Unfortunately, many people interpret it as meaning you should try to resolve the disagreement before you go to sleep. Even if you come to some sort of resolution, the damage done to your relationship is just not worth it. One reason so much damage is done is because your brain is like a muscle in that it requires a lot of energy to function properly. If you are tired or hungry, your brain is not able to perform to the best of its ability. Wait until you are well fed and well rested to continue the discussion, and you will find it will be much easier to resolve the disagreement.

5. Be respectful and use a respectful tone of voice. If the phone rings during a heated conversation, both you and your spouse know whoever answers the phone will do so using a respectful tone of voice. If you have enough self-control to do that for someone who may be a complete stranger, why not make an extra effort to provide that same courtesy for your spouse?

Take the time to write down a specific plan for what you will do differently the next time you find yourself in a disagreement with your spouse.

How will being satisfied with our marriage now insure that we will be satisfied with our marriage later?

Growing Back Together Again

The Dallen's house was full of pots. There were pots on every conceivable flat surface. Tall, straight ones and short, fat curvy pots covered in polka dots, glazed and unglazed, purposefully ugly ones and unexpectedly beautiful pots. The ones near the doorways inevitably had little knick-knacks in them, loose change and twisty ties, or the receipts they did not think to throw away. There were even several full of blue buttons. Mr. Dallen, until very recently, had worked at the button factory and would bring home a few of the basic, four-hole, blue buttons every week or so. He would keep them in odd places around his room. But when he had bought his wife the studio and she had started to make pots, he just decided to gather them all together in a pot here and a pot there. And because there were so many pots, Mrs. Dallen never knew that any of them had any buttons in them.

The reason there were so many pots was because Mrs. Dallen had just become a ceramic artist. She was not very good yet, and she did not really know if it was appropriate to try and sell her pots, whose purposes were primarily decorative. So, she placed them around the house in anticipation of the day when she would know what to do with them.

Mr. Dallen did not mind. He had bought her the

studio so she could make things with clay, something she had wanted to do for their entire marriage. Now that the children were out of the house, and the property Mr. and Mrs. Dallen had bought in Texas early on in their marriage was full of oil, they both had the time and money to do the things that had eluded them for so long. So Mr. Dallen retired and furnished a complete, if somewhat smallish, ceramic studio for his wife on the back of their house.

As they were shopping for used kilns and ceramics wheels, (Mrs. Dallen was still frugal, even if they had become rich, and insisted on starting with used equipment) Mr. Dallen tried to think of what he would do with his free time now that his wife was going to be a ceramic artist. He decided he would try to get into this new video game craze. He had seen the ones his son had played and thought maybe there was something a little tamer, more his pace. While his wife was discussing types of clay with a shopkeeper, he went to the electronics store and perused the game systems. He left a half hour later with an older game system, one that would attach to his TV, and a few games, including *Dr. Stickit's Stamp Collecting Challenge* and *Chicken Hatcher*. Mr. Dallen was pleased with his purchases.

Thus, Mr. and Mrs. Dallen entered into two separate retirements: Mr. Dallen with his video games and Mrs. Dallen with her studio. They made an effort to eat at least one meal together during the day, but Mrs. Dallen liked to get up early and Mr. Dallen liked to sleep in, so breakfast was out. In fact, Mrs. Dallen got up so early, and Mr. Dallen so late, that her lunch was only an hour after his "breakfast."

They did eat dinner together every weeknight. They watched their two favorite game shows and ate, only making comments about the game or certain contestants.

> What is stopping you from giving your spouse a hug that lasts at least a minute everyday?

They never talked about each other's day or activities because they each figured they knew what their spouse was doing. Any detail he or she could give would not be worth sharing with the other, only moderately interested partner. And so after that hour of dismal interaction, they went back to their respective parts of the house. Mrs. Dallen spent the time cleaning up the studio and preparing for the next morning before going to bed. Mr. Dallen stayed up for three more hours reading and watching his news show.

Neither of them noticed how predictable it all was, and neither of them noticed how far apart they had grown. Mr. and Mrs. Dallen each felt that they still loved their partner, but that fact was just understood. They need not go out of their way to encourage affection or express their feelings. They had been growing apart since the children were born. Mr. Dallen worked long hours at the button factory and Mrs. Dallen always had the children to take to school, soccer or piano. Time for themselves had been put on a shelf somewhere and forgotten about, as neither of them thought it a necessity. This negligence to their relationship might have continued spiraling downward if someone had not brought it to Mr. Dallen's attention.

Mr. and Mrs. Lisbon had been neighbors of the Dallens for many years before they retired and moved to a condominium in Florida. Mrs. Lisbon and Mrs. Dallen still kept in contact, as women often do. Mrs. Lisbon would tell

Mrs. Dallen about playing golf with Mr. Lisbon and how much fun it was spending time with her sweetie. Mrs. Dallen would smile over the phone encouragingly and make "mhmmm"ing noises to show she was listening, even though she wasn't really. But Mrs. Lisbon wasn't a very skilled phone converser, and so she wouldn't notice Mrs. Dallen's lukewarm confirmations. Consequently, when Mrs. Lisbon mentioned that they would be coming back to town for a few days next week and would it be all right to stop in for a visit, Mrs. Dallen didn't even realize the request and gave her usual "mhmmm" noise. And Mrs. Lisbon, not really listening either, heard the affirmative response and planned the visit into their trip.

So a few weeks later Mr. and Mrs. Lisbon stopped by the house and a very surprised Mr. Dallen met them at the door.

"Well, look who it is." Mr. Dallen said, extending his hand, "Mrs. Dallen is out…buying glaze or something or other, but you can come in. Would you like something to drink?" Mr. and Mrs. Lisbon entered with the traditional "hello, good to see you" and settled in the front room, the only room not filled to the gills with ceramic creations.

After the initial questions about what brought them out this way again, Mr. Lisbon asked about what the Dallens did with all their spare time.

"Well," Mr. Dallen began, "I've bought myself a game system and am having fun trying to figure out these video game things. I have one where I am a rare stamp collector and another where I raise chickens to sell. Other than that, I do most of the same things I did before."

"I see, sounds good." Mr. Lisbon replied, "And how about your wife? Does she play too?"

"You mean Tabitha? No no, she works in her studio

> Does it really matter who says "I'm sorry first"?

most of the day." Mr. Dallen told them.

"All day? What does she do in there?" Mrs. Lisbon asked.

"I guess she makes pots…I don't rightly know about all the little doodads she uses or anything…" Mr. Dallen finished lamely.

"Has she read any good books lately?"

"Ummm, not that I know of…"

Mr. and Mrs. Lisbon looked at each other awkwardly and asked to see some of her pieces in order to change the subject. They all made small talk for a few minutes more before they realized Mrs. Dallen wasn't coming home anytime soon and the Lisbons had to be going. They exchanged good-byes and left Mr. Dallen to deal with the realization he didn't know his own wife.

Mr. Dallen immediately sat down with a legal pad and a pen and began to write what he did know. He knew her birthday was September 8th and she was 49 years old. She liked ceramics and getting up early. He was pretty sure she had hazel eyes and that her original hair color was a dark blondish kind of shade. After that, he was at a loss. He couldn't remember her favorite color, if she had ever wanted pets, other hobbies she might have, or what kind of movies she liked. He was very distraught. How could this have happened? They had been so in love when they got married. While they were courting, they saw each other every minute they weren't working or asleep. They talked all the time about every possible subject, and now, not only had he forgotten a lot of what he used to know about her, he didn't remember anything current about her either. "This is, indeed, quite the pickle," thought Mr. Dallen. "Something must be done."

When Mrs. Dallen came home that evening from all her errands, Mr. Dallen was waiting outside the house in a shirt and tie. As she came up the walk, Mr. Dallen took her hand, kissed it and said, "Hello, my dear." Mrs. Dallen was completely taken aback and giggled as she hadn't for many years. "Why don't you go put on a nice dress," Mr. Dallen continued, "I'd like to take you on a date." Mrs. Dallen dropped her shopping bag inside the door and was ready in ten minutes. During dinner she tried to figure out what all this was about. Mr. Dallen did not explain about the Lisbons coming to visit or how embarrassed he was that he didn't know more about his wife, but he did say, "I want to get to know my sweetie again. Tell me things."

As the evening went on, they both drew in the words and actions of the other, remembering their early days together. Mr. Dallen noticed Mrs. Dallen's eyes were brown with golden circles in the middle, and Mrs. Dallen remembered why she fell in love in the first place. They both realized photography was something they were interested in, and decided to take a class together. As they finished dinner, Mr. Dallen leaned into his wife, taking her hand. "Please don't let it be so long before I get to know you again" he said.

"I won't if you won't" she told him, smiling.

They both knew they still wanted to be together, and while they would have to take time to be together, it was time well spent.

Ounce of Prevention Worksheet

Being married is like going up a river in a canoe. You are either paddling together and progressing towards your destination, paddling against each other and going in circles or not paddling enough and drifting backwards. Unfortunately in the river of marriage, if we drift too long we will find ourselves in a set of rapids that can quickly take us over the falls of divorce.

Many couples find that they get into a comfortable routine and become satisfied with slowly drifting. It is only over time they realize they have been drifting apart. By the time they realize this, many think it is too late and nothing can be done. In almost all cases this is simply not true. With enough time and effort almost every couple can not only grow closer together, but, once they have closed that distance, will find that their marriage is stronger than ever before. The key, though, is time, effort and consistency.

The first step to getting back on track is finding extra time you can use to spend with your spouse. Track how you spend your time each week. Select several of the items on the list you are willing to sacrifice in order to spend more time with your spouse. The sacrifice may seem difficult at first but the benefits to your marriage will far outweigh any costs.

The second step is to turn that extra time you are sacrificing into quality time with your spouse. An obvious choice would be to set aside time for a weekly date. Brainstorm ideas with your spouse on quality dates you can go on in the next few weeks. Another idea is to schedule time each day to reconnect by just talking. If you don't have children, then eating meals together can be a great time. If you do have children, then setting aside 10-15 minutes after dinner works as well. Don't get caught in the trap that you need to set aside large blocks of time. Giving a hug or a kiss that lasts for a minute or making a quick call just to say hi can make a significant difference over time.

Start making a list right now of what you can do to increase the quantity and quality of the time you spend with your spouse every day and each week. Then brainstorm with your spouse other items you can add to the list.

The most important step is to not let anything or anyone prevent you from spending more quality time with your spouse. By making this small sacrifice now, you can maintain a healthy and happy marriage that will bring you all of the benefits associated with healthy marriages.

Who benefits when you hold on to anger?

Why Can't You Just Say "I Love You"?

"That's it!" Lacey yelled, yanking her coat off the wooden hook by the door. "What is your problem? Why can't you just *say* 'I love you,' huh? I say it all the time and all I get in return is a 'Right back at ya' or something stupid like that. We've been married two years. Do you love me or not?" She stood in front of the door still holding her coat with her hands on her hips, daring him to answer otherwise.

"Me! What about you?" James retorted. "You never *do* anything for me. How am I supposed to know that you love me?" He threw up his hands in frustration. "Have you ever considered that your 'I love you' doesn't mean that much to me?"

Stunned and hurt, Lacey glanced at James then at the floor, put on her coat, and quietly walked out the door.

James sat down on the black leather couch, elbows on his knees, and forehead resting in his hands. They had been having this argument since a few months after they were married, and he still did not get it. What was the big deal about him not saying "I love you" very often? They were just words to James. He thought back to his family and tried to remember if they said "I love you." He thought for a moment. There were not many instances he could remember, but he knew they loved each other. He remembered surprising his sister by making her bed while she was in the shower or making his dad's favorite breakfast on his birthday. James also remembered his dad occasionally bringing flowers home for his mother or surprising her with a small gift—just because. "Yes," he thought. "We knew we were loved because of those special moments, because of the things we were willing to do for each other." Thinking about it made him even more frustrated. He had tried all those things with Lacey, but she never seemed to appreciate it like he anticipated. Getting angrier by the minute, James lay down on the couch, hoping he could sleep off the surge of emotion coursing through his body.

Lacey pulled into a parking lot, turned off the ignition and banged her fist on the steering wheel. James was so difficult. All she wanted was a simple "I love you" and it would start World War III! How could he be so stubborn and so hurtful? She rested her head on the steering wheel and began to cry softly. "My 'I love you' means nothing?" she whispered the question into the silence. She watched the children playing in the park while mulling over her thoughts. Another half-hour passed before Lacey slowly started her way back home. She and James needed some help, and it seemed their only option was counseling. Lacey had heard somewhere that some couples often took as long as six years after trouble started to seek help, but by then it was usually too late. Lacey didn't want to be one of those couples. They would have to start to fix the problem now—hopefully.

When Lacey arrived home, James was still peacefully sleeping on the couch. She went over, sat down on the floor next to him, and gently started running her

> What are you doing to prevent telling your children that you and your spouse "just don't love each other anymore"

fingers through his hair. The anger had passed and she lovingly looked at the man she'd promised to spend her life with. More than anything, Lacey wanted a happily ever after. She was willing to put in the effort she knew it would take. James began to stir and slowly opened his eyes to look at Lacey. After a minute or two, Lacey decided to break the comfortable silence.

"James, I'm sorry," there was a gentle tone to her voice now; "I don't mean to get so upset. It's just that it would mean so much to me to hear you say those words. It also seems like there's something you need from me that keeps bothering you, and I don't know what it is. Maybe we should talk to someone and try to get some help."

Lacey was still running her fingers through James' hair and down the side of his face. He looked up at her and saw how sincere she was. He thought for a moment, then finally said, "I guess that would be alright. You just have to promise me if it doesn't start helping us soon, then we can stop going. Okay?"

"Deal."

Two weeks later James and Lacey were sitting in Dr. Singer's waiting room. Together they had decided that after a month, if they were not seeing any benefit to counseling, then they would stop, possibly find another counselor or just quit all together.

"Come right on in you two," Dr. Singer was holding

open the office door. "Go ahead and have a seat and tell me a little bit about what's worrying you two."

James and Lacey sat down on the couch and proceeded to tell the therapist how they had a hard time feeling the other person truly loved them, and when they discussed the matter it usually ended in conflict.

Dr. Singer gave a slight smile, and there seemed to be a little twinkle in his eye. "It may or may not surprise you that a lot of couples deal with this same type of struggle. Let me first explain why, and then we'll talk about some solutions. Sound good?"

James and Lacey nodded their heads.

"Good. Obviously you have both come from different families, and in those families you learned how to express love differently. From what you have both told me it sounds like Lacey came from what I call a verbal family. Your family expressed love predominately by saying it or writing little notes to each other and things like that. Correct me if I'm wrong."

Lacey slightly shook her head no.

"Now James, it appears you come from a visual family. Don't misunderstand me. I don't mean you notice perfect body figures or that Lacey has to have her make-up and hair done perfectly every day. What I'm saying is that you notice things she does specifically for you; for example, if she made the bed, made your favorite breakfast, or swept up the floor in your work shop for you. Right?"

James nodded in the affirmative.

"The third type is touch. These people like a hug and a kiss on their way out the door, holding their partner's hand while walking down the street, or just being close by them. Everyone is generally a mix of all three, but it seems that you, Lacey, are predominantly verbal and you, James, are visual. Now, here is the solution. You have to practice

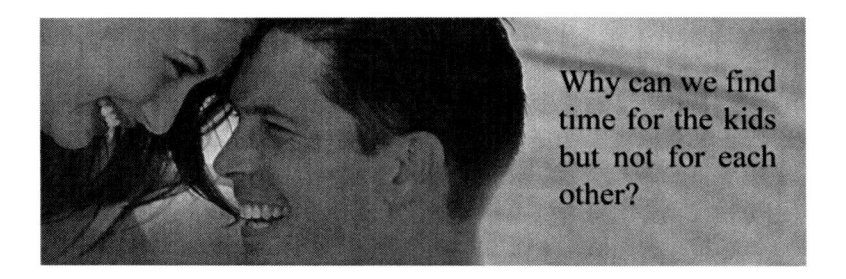

> Why can we find time for the kids but not for each other?

using each other's love languages. Not only do you have to practice them, but you must be able to start acknowledging that what your partner does in their language still means 'I love you.' Lacey, next time James surprises you by picking up dinner on his way home from work, say to yourself, 'He is trying to show me how much he loves me.' That way you will begin to see his acts as acts of love. It's not easy, but do you think you can do it?"

"But Dr. Singer," said James a little hesitantly, "what if it doesn't work, and we aren't able to speak each other's languages?"

"The only thing that would keep you from speaking the other language is yourself. It's hard at first, but if you do it, you may be surprised at how much verbal affection starts to mean to you. How about you, Lacey?"

"Why sure, I'm willing to try, but I'm just worried I won't be able to recognize enough things to do for James. Since I don't usually pay attention to those things how do I know what will mean something to him or not?"

"That is a great question Lacey, and it leads me to my last bit of advice. You also need to show appreciation to each other for attempts to speak the other person's language. The two of you should think of a signal like a purposeful touch on the arm or actually saying 'It really means a lot to me when you ....' That way, Lacey, you will know when you've done something that really speaks to

James and be able to take note of it. Alright, how about we meet back in a week, and you tell me how it goes?" They both agreed, thanked Dr. Singer, and headed home.

They struggled with Dr. Singer's challenge, but they persisted. It was three weeks before they had *any* good news to report to him.

James and Lacey were back on the plush green couch in Dr. Singer's office. They were sitting a little closer then normal, he noted. Placing his hands behind his head, Dr. Singer relaxed a bit into his own comfortable chair. "I know it's been a struggle, but you both have been working hard, and I anticipate that today you might have some positive feedback for me. James, how about you go first."

"Okay." He settled back comfortably in the couch, "I have to admit I was skeptical at first, but you were right. Things still aren't perfect or anything, but they are getting a lot better. It seems like Lacey is generally happier, and I feel more secure in our relationship. I feel like I now know how Lacey really feels about me. It'ss kind of strange, but I think I'm also starting to appreciate verbal affection a little more, like you said I would."

"Good. Good. I'm glad to hear it. What about you Lacey?"

"I agree with everything James said. I don't think I've ever been happier in our marriage." Dr. Singer continued speaking, but Lacey wasn't really listening. That morning she had received a short, but heart-felt note lying on her pillow when she stepped out of the shower. It was from James who had already left for work. She knew it was hard for him to express himself in words, which made the note mean even more. Lacey had had a pleasant rest of the day. James had come home from work tired and a little frazzled from a particularly hard day at work. It was then Lacey had decided to make his favorite meal as soon as they got home to see if it would help lift his spirits a little.

She looked over at James, smiled, and gave his hand a quick three squeezes. It was their subtle sign of affirmation that Dr. Singer had encouraged them to think of. It meant "I love you." How dearly she loved this man who had been willing to work so hard to repair their marriage. James looked over and winked at his wife.

"It was a hard lesson to learn," James mused, "but we are so much happier now that we can recognize each other's love language. We just had to be willing to make the sacrifice."

Ounce of Prevention Worksheet

While love is an action verb, the action it takes is not always the same for everyone, nor is it always recognized by everyone. The bottom line is we all express love differently than our spouses. For some couples, the differences are minor, but for other couples the differences are so great they don't even recognize the other spouses efforts.

One style of how to express love isn't necessarily better than another, while a healthy mix of each style is common. The problem is when your spouse doesn't recognize your efforts to express the love you feel for him or her.

The good news is that this problem can be overcome with time and effort. The steps may seem simple, but the positive impact on your marriage is well worth the time and effort to take them.

1. Write down the things your family did to let each other know you loved each other.

2. Write down the things you do to let your spouse know you love him or her.

3. Ask your spouse to do the same.

4. Now sit down and compare your lists.

5. After you have compared your lists, take the next three weeks to recognize each time your spouse expresses love to you.

6. After three weeks are over and you have become comfortable recognizing how your spouse expresses love, take the next three weeks to use his or her methods to express love back to your spouse.

By the end of the six weeks , you should not only be able to recognize when your spouse is expressing love toward you, but you should also be able to express love back to your spouse in a way he or she will understand.

Bonus Section
Healthy Marriage Pamphlet Series

We have also developed a series of pamphlets that can teach you additional skills and insights to form and sustain a healthy marriage. We have included the first pamphlet on *Persistence* in this book. You can read the other pamphlets at HealthyMarriageTips.com.

Persistence

What would happen if you bought a package of seeds but never planted them? What would happen if you planted the seeds and then neglected them? Just like seeds, relationship skills and knowledge won't help you grow a healthy marriage until you **APPLY** them.

How often have you learned about a change that could improve your life but never made the change? Even if you begin to make the change, how often do you fail to stick with it long enough to receive all the benefits? For most people, this happens more often than they would care to admit.

Our natural tendency is to take the path of least resistance. This often means choosing not to spend time and effort making positive changes that will improve our lives. Why are some people able to overcome these tendencies and others are not? Given the right tools and good information, the difference between those who reach their goals and those who don't is **persistence**.

Why are some couples able to form healthy marriages while so many others are not? ALL couples encounter obstacles in their marriages. Those who persist in doing the things that will strengthen their marriages are the couples who succeed in forming and sustaining healthy marriages.

How do you develop persistence? To answer this question, you must first understand what powers persistence. Persistence is like an engine and motivation is the fuel. The two main sources of motivational fuel that power the engine of persistence are external and internal. External sources include rewards and fear. Internal sources include willpower and love.

External sources produce quick bursts of power, but the power only lasts for a short amount of time. Another drawback of external sources is the increased amount of fuel needed each time in order to produce the same results. One example of this principle is to think back to when you were a small child. How much work were you willing to do for a dollar? How long would you continue working if your current salary was dropped to a dollar per hour?

You can use rewards to get your persistence engine running, but as quickly as possible you should switch over to an internal source of motivational fuel. The advantage of internal sources like willpower and love is you end up with more fuel than when you began. In essence, love and willpower become a perpetual source of fuel. Ralph Waldo Emerson wrote, *"That which we persist in doing becomes easier for us to do; not that the nature of the thing itself is changed, but that our power to do is increased"*. People who maintain positive changes fuel their persistence engine with internal motivational fuels.

Another key to success is to track the performance of your persistence engine until you have formed a habit. We have developed a tool called a *Track It To Habit Log* ™ to help you accomplish this. One copy can be found at the end of this section. You can print additional copies of the log at www.HealthyMarriage.org/habitlog.htm

If you want a healthy marriage, you also need to have a plan. If you live in New York City and want to visit the Grand Canyon, then one method is to jump in a car and start driving. More likely than not you will waste time and money because you haven't taken the time to do some research and create a driving plan. As silly as this method sounds, many couples do this when they get married. They pay thousands of dollars and spend hundreds of hours preparing for the wedding, but do little to learn how to form and sustain a healthy marriage.

No matter where you are in your marital journey, taking the time to learn basic relationship skills and knowledge will significantly increase your chance of a smoother and happier journey.

As you learn healthy relationship skills, write down a plan on how you will apply them in your marriage. We have developed a tool called *Strengthening My Marriage Plan* to help you accomplish this. You can find it at the end of this section. You can also print additional copies of the plan at www.HealthyMarriage.org/myplan.htm. To keep your marriage healthy, you will need to refer to your plan often and modify it as you encounter the inevitable challenges of marriage.

If you want a healthy marriage, then you have to persist in

applying skills and knowledge that can help you form and sustain a healthy marriage. Don't allow anything or anyone, including yourself, to keep you from persisting in strengthening your marriage.

Action Plan

1. Read the other topics in this series by going to www.HealthyMarriageTips.com

2. Take a marriage education class. For a list of classes near you, go to www.SmartMarriages.com

3. Fill out your *Strengthening My Marriage Plan*.

4. Choose a specific relationship skill to work on and use the *Track It To Habit Log* ™

5. Make a commitment to persist and not give up when times get hard.

No marriage is healthy all of the time. However, there are marriages that are healthy most of the time. When you find your marriage has become unhealthy, ask yourself, "What can I do to help my marriage become healthy again?" Don't ever wait for your spouse to take the first step to heal your marriage. Do what YOU need to do and DO IT NOW!!! The sooner you take action and apply what you have learned, the sooner your marriage can heal.

Track It To Habit Log (TM)

If you want to develop a habit, then you first need to create a Habit Plan.

1. What specific habit do you want to develop?

2. What will you do to develop this habit?

3. What obstacles might you face and how will you overcome them?

The next step is to track your habit. Untracked habits tend to quickly become forgotten goals.

Rate yourself each day on a scale of 1-10 on how well you implemented your Habit Plan. Also rate yourself on how close you are to firmly establishing your new habit. After five straight days of perfect 10s you no longer need to track your habit on a daily basis. Every six months track your habit for one week to ensure you are maintaining it. A new habit is developed on average in 30 days.

Date	Plan	Habit	Date	Plan	Habit

Date	Plan	Habit	Date	Plan	Habit

If needed, answer the following questions each night. What parts of my Habit Plan are not working?

Why might they not be working?

What can I do differently to make my Habit Plan successful?

Strengthening My Marriage Plan

"Dreams take their first step toward reality when you write them down."

1. Describe in detail the type of marriage you would be happy and satisfied with.

2. Ghandi said, *"Be the change you want to see in the world."* To form and sustain a healthy marriage you will need to *"Be the change you want to see in your marriage."* What are the specific relationships skills you need to develop to form and sustain a healthy marriage?

3. What other specific changes do you need to make to form and sustain a healthy marriage?

4. What obstacles may prevent you from forming and sustaining a healthy marriage?

5. What will you do to overcome those obstacles?

You can't follow a plan you don't remember. Review your plan on a weekly basis. Ask yourself what is working and what isn't. Be flexible and modify your plan as needed to overcome the obstacles that you will encounter.

Your signature on this contract represents your commitment to persist in fulfilling your part in strengthening your marriage.

Signature _____ Date _____

Appreciation Journal

If you only only choose to do one activity from this book, we recommend you choose this one. This activity is like Miracle-Gro for relationships. It can take relationships that are struggling and help them to thrive or it can take great relationships and make them even better.

The activity is actually very simple. Each day spend at least five minutes writing down all the things your spouse did that day that you appreciated. If you can't think of any, then take a stroll down memory lane and write about things he or she has done in the past. At the end of the day choose two-three items from your list and verbally let your spouse know how much you appreciated what was done.

Continue this activity for at least thirty days and you should witness a miraculous change in your relationship.

The rest of the blank pages of this book have been included for you to start your *Appreciation Journal*.

_____
_____
_____
_____
_____
_____
_____
_____
_____
_____

RESOURCE LIST

ON BASE

AIRMEN & FAMILY READINESS CENTER (A&FRC) 828-2458
The core function of the Airman and Family Readiness Center (AFRC) is to help families and individuals enhance their quality of life, learn how to adapt the changes and demands of military life. A&FRC goal is to link individuals and families with the right resources to meet their specific needs.

> **Family Life Education and Consultation:** A variety of programs are offered to help families adapt to the military lifestyle. These can be taken as a class or through one-on-one consultation.
>
> - **7 Habits of Highly Effective Families** – Learn how to apply the 7 Habits of Highly Effective People to your family relationships and find the answers to challenges faced in the military family.
>
> - **Four Lenses Personality Discovery** – Learn the mystery of your own behaviors and recognizing and encouraging potential in others. Learn to use this invaluable tool to bridge the gaps in communication within your career, with your family, and in personal relationships. Only when we understand, can we change.
>
> - **Heart Link** - Learn to adjust, adapt and belong to the Air Force family. This fun,

interactive and informative program gives spouses the tools to understand and navigate through the Air Force mission, customs, traditions, and support services. With the Heart Link advantage you have the tools to take care of yourself, family and community.

- **Laugh Your Way to a Better Marriage** – Based on Mark Gungor's wildly popular seminar, Laugh Your Way to a Better Marriage® this video based education program uses a unique blend of humor and tell-it-like-it-is honesty to help couples get along and have fun doing it.

- **Love and Logic** – Learn to raise kids who are self-confident, motivated, and ready for the real world—without resorting to anger, threats, nagging, or exhausting power struggles.

- **Marriage Wellness** – Learn specific marriage communication skills such as saying what you want and getting what you want. These new skills can help enhance any special relationship.

- **Parenting with 1-2-3 Magic** – Learn how to handle difficult behavior, encourage good behavior, and mange the inevitable sidetrack of testing and manipulation of children 2-12 years with some simple, precise and effective methods.

- **PREP Workshop** – Learn skills and principles of successful relationships. Say what you need to say, get to the heart o f problems and increase your connection with each other.

- **Pre-deployment Briefing** - Mandatory briefing for AD members leaving for more than 30 days. Discussing how the A&FRC can support them during their TDY, deployment, or remote assignment. Highly encourage spouses to attend. No appointment needed.

- **Surviving your Teens** – Learn how to manage and let go of your 13-18 year olds. Master some practical guidelines for handling the complex situations and dilemmas that teenagers often present.

- **Time Management** – Learn how to identify and prioritize the most important things in your life so you accomplish tasks, reach goals, and focus on the really important parts of life.

- **Understanding Combat Stress** – Gain an understanding of actions and reactions that are healthy in the combat zone but are no longer needed back home. Learn why it often takes time to readjust back to normal. and why certain environments or experiences can trigger combat reactions, what can be done to help reduce the triggers, and when referral to experts may be needed.

Financial Counseling: Whether you have need for personal assistance with a one-on-one appointment to help develop a solution for your financial issues or just want to increase your knowledge in financial management we have the resources for you.

- **Common Cents Money Management** – Learn to put your financial house in order, find hidden spending, keep more of what you make, and other skills that help you achieve financial independence.

- **Credit When Credit is Due** – This six week course helps individuals gain a basic understanding of money issues and their responsibilities revolving around the world of credit. Individuals who successfully complete the course will become better risks in the eyes of lenders and should be better prepared to handle their personal finances in the future.

- **Managing Your Credit Score** – Managing your credit is more important and more complicated than ever. With good credit, you can get a bigger house, a better car, a lower credit card rate and less-costly insurance. Without it, you'll always have a drag on your finances – and that means fewer of the things you want. Learn how to establish credit, improve your credit, and get out of credit debt.

- **Saving and Investing in Your Future** - Start planning for your future with the money you make today. It's never too early or too late to start saving or investing and the longer your money is working for you, the greater your return will be. Learn about the various types of savings and investment options and how to work them into your financial future.

- **TSP Workshop-** TSP can be a great option for civil service and military members looking to put money aside for retirement. Learn about the various funds, and how to estimate what you would need to put away for your future.

Air Force Aid Society (AFAS): The AFAS offers emergency financial assistance when a bona fide need exists for qualified personnel. Examples of financial emergencies might be airfare when a close family member is very ill or has died, payment for repairs to a family's only car, or help purchasing groceries when there is a financial crisis. Level of assistance is determined on a case by case basis.

School Liaison: Based in the Airman & Family Readiness Center, the School Liaison (SL) is available to act as a liaison for parents and students with the goal of helping schools and government agencies share best practices and policies, and serve as an advocate for military families to make sure children and youth are not being penalized in school by their families' service to our nation whether you are new to the base, getting ready to PCS to a new duty station, or you have an Exceptional Family Member and want to know what community resources are available for your family, the School Liaison is here to inform, connect and advocate for military families.

Chapel 828-6417

Chaplains offer counseling for alcoholism, drugs, family, premarital or marital problems, moral issues, conscientious objector status, work related, and other areas of concern. You have total confidentiality. The chaplains cannot share any information with anyone without your permission.

Family Advocacy Program (FAP) 828-7520

FAP is dedicated to helping families prevent and treat any and all maltreatment issues and concerns. Programs and services provided through FAP include:

- **Baby Care Basics** – Take the first steps in parenting. Learn the essentials of basic care and safety for that new member of the family, whether this is your first or second child.

- **Dad's Class** – A class for Dad's taught by Dad's. Learn about the joys and fears of becoming a new dad.

- **Family Advocacy Safety Education Seminar (FASES)** - A four hour seminar designed to enhance individual, couple and family functioning thru awareness of interpersonal patterns (anger management, communication, parenting).

- **Marital Counseling**

- **Sibling Class** – Learn to understand and deal with the unique relationship of siblings, and teach older children ages 2 and up on

Ounce of Prevention HealthyMarriageTips.com

what to expect when the baby arrives.

HEALTH AND WELLNESS CENTER (HAWC) 828-7417
The Health and Wellness Center is dedicated to prevention and health enhancement. It is a "one stop" shop for health and fitness assessment, awareness, prevention intervention programs, and exercise prescriptions.

MENTAL HEALTH 828-7580
Mental health offers coping skills training classes and individual counseling to help with such problems as depression, anxiety, and adjustment difficulties. Services are available to Gunfighters and their families.

- **Anger Management** - Unmanaged anger destroys relationships, families, and individual health. Learn to understand and control your responses to anger. Must attend six consecutive weeks to receive a certificate.
- **Group Therapy**
- **Individual therapy** (psychotherapy and limited psycho-pharmacology)
- **Relaxation Group** - This is held as a 3 session group that meets each Friday. Contact Mental Health to find out when the next 3 class session begins.
- **Stress Management** - Your ability to cope with stress increases as you learn and adopt more coping skills. It is like money in the bank to weather tough times, the more you

have, the better you can deal with the uncertainties of life.

MILITARY FAMILY LIFE CONSULTANT (MFLC)
208-598-5974

MFLCs are available through A&FRC for short term, situational, problem-solving counseling sessions free of charge. MFLCs provide psycho-education to help military service members and their families understand the impact of stress, deployments, family reunions following deployments and the stresses of the military lifestyle. They are here to augment existing military support services. Services can be provided on or off base and can be provided to individuals, couples, families and groups. MFLCs are mandated reporters of child abuse, domestic violence, and duty to warn situations; services are otherwise private.

IN THE COMMUNITY

211 IDAHO CARE LINE
DIAL 211 OR 1-800-926-2588
An option for obtaining Idaho specific information. You can also access the 211 Idaho informational database online at www.idahocareline.org and click on the 211 link.

AUTISM SOCIETY OF AMERICA, TREASURE VALLEY
CHAPTER WWW.ASATVC.ORG
Free monthly speaker meetings the first Monday of every month at St Luke's Medical Center (Eagle, Idaho). Provides Information about Services and Programs in the

Treasure Valley and participates in Legislative Advocacy. Email: Autism.asatvc@yahoo.com and request to be added to our email list. (208) 336-5676 message phone.

DEPLOYMENT INFO FOR KIDS
DEPLOYMENTLINK.OSD.MIL/KIDSLINK/INTRO.HTM

GIVE AN HOUR   WWW.GIVEANHOUR.ORG
A non-profit organization where mental health professionals nationwide volunteer to donate an hour of time each week to military personnel and families affected by the conflicts in Iraq and Afghanistan. You can search for providers in your community.

IDAHO ASPERGER'S SUPPORT GROUP
WWW.IDAHOASG.ORG
The Idaho Asperger's Support Group is based in Boise, Idaho. Meetings are held monthly on the second Thursday of the month. A teen group meets weekly. We are dedicated to providing support for those affected by Asperger's Syndrome and other high-functioning autism spectrum disorders. In addition, we welcome and encourage educators, medical professionals and anyone interested in learning more about Asperger's Syndrome to join in. Email: amy@idahoasg or nicole@idahoasg.

IDAHO AUTISM   IDAHOAUTISM.COM
(IA) is a online resource guide. Find information for support groups, activities for families with an autistic child and the latest news and treatment information.

Idaho Parent's Unlimited, Inc
www.ipulidaho.org   1-800-242-4785

Idaho Parents Unlimited, Inc. supports, empowers, educates and advocates enhancing the quality of life for Idahoans with disabilities and their families. Email: parents@ipulidaho.org

MILITARY CHILD EDUCATION
WWW.MILITARYCHILD.ORG

MILITARY CHILD EDUCATION COALITION
WWW.MILITARYCHILD.ORG

MILITARY MOMS
WWW.MILITARYMOMS.NET

MILITARY ONE SOURCE
WWW.MILITARYONESOURCE.COM   1-800-342-9647

You can access One Source consultants 24 hours a day, 7 days a week, 365 days a year. Or you can go online to access information or email a consultant. One Source programs are provided in partnership with A&FRC.

MILITARY LIVING PUBLICATIONS
WWW.MILITARYLIVING.COM

NATIONAL DOMESTIC VIOLENCE HOTLINE
1-800-799-7233

NATIONAL MILITARY FAMILY ASSOCIATION
WWW.NMFA.ORG

SPECIALIZED TRAINING OF MILITARY PARENTS
WWW.STOMPPROJECT.ORG

Made in the USA